Where is Lonely?

Acknowledgements

I wish to thank Maria Moloney, Stuart Davies, Trevor Greenfield, John Hunt and all at Our Street Books and John Hunt publishing for making this book possible.

Especial thanks to my dear friend Andrea Davies-Miller for her advice, support and encouragement for this project, and also to my lovely cousin Vanessa Britton for her expertise and generous help with the teaching notes.

Thank you to darling Rose Seren Williams for giving her approval to the illustrations in a manner that only a three-year-old can.

This book is dedicated to my Spirit Daughter
Rose Seren Williams
Dare to be different, always be yourself.
With much love always
Eva x

This is a story about Chelsea who is Lonely

and Lonely who is grumpy,

and how becoming friends

changes everything.

Who is Chelsea?

Chelsea has loads of energy.
  She has a big

  She never sits still.
  Chelsea is six years old.

Sometimes she fidgets so much that her granddad shakes
his head and says, 'Chelsea, you've got ants in your pants.'

At school Miss Hartley sighs. 'Chelsea, you need to sit down and do your work.'

Chelsea finds school difficult.

All the sitting still.

All the concentrating.

Except for nature studies.
Chelsea loves nature studies because she loves animals.
Big animals.
Small animals.
Birds.
Mice.
Insects.

Chelsea likes to be friends with animals.

The other children in the class scream when they see a spider but Chelsea loves spiders. She thinks the children are silly to be afraid of something so small.

Sometimes the boys in the playground call her names. Chelsea chases them and tries to hit them with a stick. This gets her into trouble but she doesn't think it's fair.

The girls won't play with Chelsea. They say she's like a boy with all her running around and climbing.

At home when she wants to run and jump, her mum and dad say, 'Come and sit down and watch the telly, Chelsea.'

All her life Chelsea couldn't understand why grownups would want to sit down indoors all the time.

Why didn't they want to be outdoors?

watching spiders *scuttle* across the pavement,

smelling the f l o w e r s

f e e l i n g the soft grass

and listening to

It was so much more exciting.

Where is Lonely?

Eva McIntyre

**OUR STREET
BOOKS**

Winchester, UK
Washington, USA

First published by Our Street Books, 2014
Our Street Books is an imprint of John Hunt Publishing Ltd., Laurel House, Station Approach,
Alresford, Hants, SO24 9JH, UK
office1@jhpbooks.net
www.johnhuntpublishing.com
www.ourstreet-books.com

For distributor details and how to order please visit the 'Ordering' section on our website.

Text copyright: Eva McIntyre 2013

ISBN: 978 1 78099 868 8

A CIP catalogue record for this book is available from the British Library.

Design: Stuart Davies

Printed and bound by CPI Group (UK) Ltd, Croydon, CR0 4YY

We operate a distinctive and ethical publishing philosophy in all
areas of our business, from our global network of authors to
production and worldwide distribution.

Chelsea woke up after a lovely sleep.

She was always first to wake up in her house.

It was Saturday and Saturday was Chelsea's favourite day.

Her mum and dad always had a lie-in, and her brother was in his room, playing on his iPad as usual.

So Chelsea got up before everyone else
and crept d
          o
            w
              n
                 s
                   t
                  a
                  i
                   r
                  s

so that they wouldn't hear her.

She went into the kitchen and made some jam sandwiches. She wrapped them in foil and popped them in her pocket. Chelsea loved jam sandwiches and she ate them every day.

Then she sneaked out through the back door.

Once she was outside, she ran down the lane and into the countryside, laughing and shouting, 'Woooo, woooo!'

It was  Spr ing and spring was Chelsea's favourite
time of year because of all the new things growing.

Well spring was her favourite time of year until

ummer

came, then summer was her favourite because there was
so much more time to run around.

Then

Au Tumn

was her favourite because of the colours of the leaves.
Then

W 1 nter

because of the snow.

Every time of year was Chelsea's favourite.

But this day it was spring and the daffodils were dancing in the breeze.

Birds were collecting bits and pieces to make their nests.

Squirrels were scampering into gardens to take nuts from bird feeders and bury them in the ground.

Chelsea stretched and sighed. 'What a lovely day,' she said to herself.

Then she took in a big deep breath that went right down to her toes and sent her giggling across the field and into the woods.

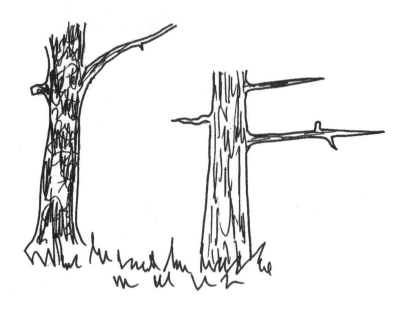

Chelsea looked up. The tall trees reached far above her.

Their leaves were beginning to grow so that the sun had to squeeze round them to reach down and touch the ground.

Chelsea looked down. The bluebells were beginning to poke their heads through the earth to see whether it was warm enough to come out. Chelsea found a beetle crawling over some old, dead branches and bent down to watch it.

Suddenly, she heard the strangest sound. 'Urgh! Urgh! Drat!'

Chelsea followed the sound through the woods until she came to an open space where there was a big, old oak tree beside a ditch.

And in the ditch sat a huge, green Ogre.

He was all tangled up in ivy, and no matter how hard he struggled, he couldn't get free.

Chelsea said, 'Can I help you?'

The Ogre turned and looked at her in surprise. Then he got cross.

'Go away, little girl. If you don't go away, I will yell at you,' he said fiercely.

Chelsea wasn't frightened of him very much and she was used to being yelled at, so she said, 'Go on then.'

The Ogre took a deep breath, opened his mouth to show his huge, tombstone teeth and his big, warty tongue and he YELLED!

m
u   p
j   e

The birds   d in surprise.

The squirrels TuTTed and their heads

But *Chelsea*

Laughed & Laughed & Laughed

'You call that a yell?' she said. 'Even I can do better than that.'

And to prove it, she took in a big, deep breath, opened her mouth and YELLED!

And she was right.

The birds flew up to the tops of the trees.

The squirrels put their hands over their ears.

'Where did you learn to yell like that?' asked the Ogre.

'From my dad,' said Chelsea. 'If you want to hear someone yell, he can really yell.' And to show him, she yelled and yelled and yelled.

'How can he yell so well?' asked the Ogre. 'Is he an Ogre?'

'No,' laughed Chelsea. 'He just hates his job and when he comes home, me and my brother we're always arguing, so he yells to make us stop.'

'Oh,' said the Ogre, puzzled. Then he got cross again and said, 'Anyway, go away or I will stamp my foot.'

'Go on, then,' said Chelsea.

The Ogre **wriggled** an enormous foot free from the ivy, lifted it high above the ground and brought it down with a big thud.

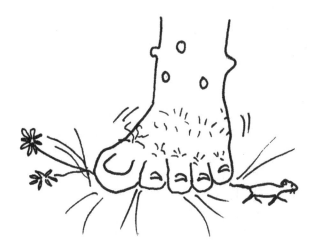

The birds bounced on the branches.
A squirrel f

      e

       l

        l

           to the floor with a surprised look on his face.

Chelsea laughed and laughed and giggled and giggled.

'You call that a stamp? Even I can do better than that,' she said.

And to prove it, she lifted her leg up high and stamped her foot down as hard as she could.

And she was right.

The ground shook.

A branch fell from the tree and landed on the ground with a crash.

'How did you learn to stamp like that?' asked the Ogre.

'From my mum,' said Chelsea. 'If you want to see someone stamp, she can really stamp.'

And to show him, she stamped and stamped and stamped.

'How can she stamp so well?' asked the Ogre. 'Is she a Witch?'

'No,' laughed Chelsea. 'She hates her job too. And when she gets home, she has to do the washing and cooking and cleaning. And me and my brother we pester her for sweets, so she stamps her foot to make us stop.'

'Oh,' said the Ogre, even more puzzled. Then he remembered to be cross and said, 'Anyway, go away or I will...I will...I will...sulk.'

'Go on then,' said Chelsea.

The Ogre was beginning to wonder about this little girl but he sat very still and concentrated very hard.

He screwed up his face so that his chin almost touched his nose and his eyebrows were hiding his eyes.

His face went red and he SULKED.

The birds stopped their singing. The hedgehogs curled up into balls to hide.

But Chelsea sat down on a tree stump and laughed and laughed and laughed.

'You call that a sulk? Even I can do better than that!'

And to prove it, she screwed up her face so tight that you couldn't see her eyes.

Her face went purple and she *SULKED*.

And she was right.
The sun hid behind a

The animals went silent.

'How did you learn to sulk like that?' asked the Ogre.

'From my brother,' said Chelsea. 'If you want to see someone sulk, he can really sulk. He can keep it up for hours.'

And to show him, she sulked and sulked and sulked.

'How can he sulk so well?' asked the Ogre. 'Is he a Troll?'

'No,' laughed Chelsea. 'He just likes to get his own way and if he doesn't, he sulks until Mum and Dad give in.'

'Oh,' said the Ogre, he was getting a little scared of this strange, little girl now.

But he acted all tough and said, 'Anyway, go away! If you don't go away, I'll burp.'

'Go on then,' said Chelsea.

The Ogre stirred up all the juices in his tummy. He sent them round and round until they were as **fizzy** as a bottle of lemonade. And then he opened his mouth and out came the biggest, smelliest BURP!

The birds flew away in disgust.

The squirrels pushed their faces into holes in the ground.

Chelsea fell off the tree stump.

She rolled on the ground and giggled and giggled and laughed and laughed.

'That is some burp,' she said. 'Even I can't do better than that.

She got up from the ground and reached into her pocket.

'But I can do something to make your breath smell nicer. Nearly as nice as cleaning your teeth.'

Chelsea opened her packet of jam sandwiches.

They were a bit squashed but still very nice.

She handed one to the Ogre.

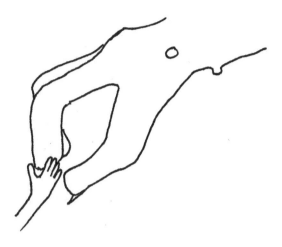

He took it from her carefully and popped it into his big mouth.

It tasted SO good.

The Ogre had never had jam sandwiches before, but he really liked them now.

'Thank you,' said the Ogre. 'But why are you being nice to me?'

'Because I want to be friends,' said Chelsea, and she held out her hand. 'My name is Chelsea, what's yours?'

The Ogre took her hand gently between his thumb and finger and said, 'Hello, Chelsea, my name is Lonely. I've never had a friend before. What do friends do?'

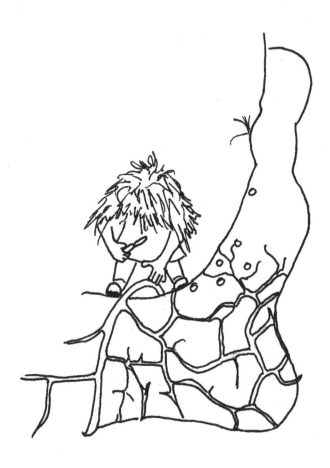

'Well,' said Chelsea.

'First of all, they have fun and never leave anyone out.

And second of all, they tell each other their secrets.

And third of all, they help each other.'

And with that, Chelsea took her penknife out of her pocket, climbed into the ditch and began to cut through the ivy until the Ogre was free.

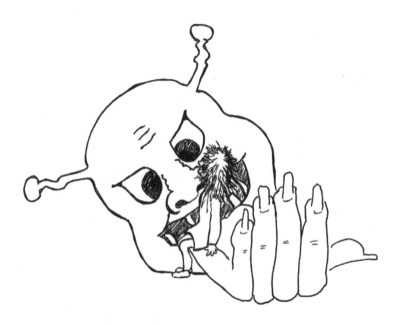

The Ogre stood up, s t r e t c h e d, and smiled. It was good to be free from the ivy. And it was good not to be left all on his own any more.

He bent down and gently picked Chelsea up so that he could look into her face.

Then he said, 'Thank you for not running away when I yelled and stamped and sulked and burped, because I think I'm going to enjoy being friends.'

'So am I,' said Chelsea. 'But we're going to have to find you a new name. You can't be called Lonely anymore because you've got a friend.'

And they
            laughed
                        and
                        laughed
                                    and
                                                laughed!

Teaching Notes

These notes are to help teachers and parents to make use of this story for a variety of educational purposes. They are aimed at Reception and Key Stage 1 children.

Story Box

Put together a box of items to use with the following activities and discussion.

Items for inclusion:

Items for making sandwiches
Photographs of seasons, forests, animals, minibeasts
Pictures of ogres
Models of animals and minibeasts
Leaves
Feathers
Fake fur
Sticks and pebbles
Seeds and bulbs
Finger puppet spiders and other creatures
A friendship bracelet
Piece of real or plastic ivy

Themes and activities

Sandwiches

Activity
Make jam sandwiches in class.

Discussion points
What could you add to a jam sandwich?
What are your favourite sandwich fillings?
Do you eat the same thing every day?
Why do we need a variety of foods in our diet?

Writing task
Write up instructions for making a jam sandwich.
Make a list of sandwich fillings.
Create your own sandwich recipe.

Art task
Draw a picture of your favourite sandwich.

Books
The Giant Jam Sandwich, John Vernon Lord and Janet Burroway
The *Sandwich Swap,* Kelly DiPucchio, Rania Al Abdullah, Tricia Tusa.

Spiders

Activity

Research how many different spiders there are and where they live.

If you have a forest school or nature area, this would make an ideal outdoor activity.

Writing tasks

Make a list of spiders

Which spiders are dangerous? Where do they live?

Write about whether we should be afraid of spiders.

Write your own story or poem about a spider.

Art task

Draw a picture of a spider to illustrate your story or poem.

Books

Spiders! Monica Molina

Spiders kids look and learn Becky Wolff

Aaargh Spider! Lydia Monks

Hairy, Scary, Spider? Paula McBride

There's a Spider in the Bath! Neil Griffiths and Peggy Collins

DVDs

Spider! I'm Only Scary 'cos I'm Hairy! 13 musical adventures about spiders and friends. Maverick Studio

Animal Nation – Spider Power, Pegasus entertainment

Animals

Activity

Explore the different types of animals with pictures, models and items from the story box and also with any school pets.

Think about difference in size and shape: fur, feathers and scales; different numbers of legs etc.

Which animals do you like best? Do you have a favourite? Why are there so many animals? Why do we need so many different animals in the world?

Writing task

List all the different types of animals in order of size
Draw some animals to show the different sizes.

Art task

Make a collage to show the different fur, scales and feathers.

Resources

CD

Wild Farm Domestic Animals Teaching Resources pack KS1 EYFS SEN SCIENCE

Book

Animals plants and habitats, KS1 Catherine Yemm

Seasons and Nature

Activities

Discover what happens in the different seasons.

Which animals do we see in which seasons?

What happens to plants and trees in different seasons? Do they all make the same changes?

Does every country in the world have the same four seasons?

Why do some birds migrate?

Nature Studies

Invite a member of your local wildlife trust to come and talk to the class.

Watch a caterpillar become a chrysalis and then change into a butterfly.

Use your forest school or nature area to look for mini beasts or look at some mini beasts brought in by your wildlife trust visitor.

Jigsaws

Mothercare. *My Layered Seasons Puzzle*, in four layers building the same picture in each season. 13 pieces each layer.

JR childrens. *Four Seasons* 4 jigsaws, Winter, Spring, Summer and Autumn. 200 pieces each for older children to work in groups.

Writing task

Write a list of all the things that change in each of the four seasons.

Write about the minibeasts you have found and where they live.

Art task

Using air-drying clay or Plasticine, make models of minibeasts.

Books

The Listening Walk, Paul Showers
Come on, Rain, Karen Hesse
Night in the Country, Cynthia Rylant and Mary Szilagyi
The Magic School Bus series, Joanna Cole and Bruce Degen

Ogres

Are ogres real? Can you think of any other stories or films about ogres?

Why is Lonely cross?
Why do you think he's called 'Lonely'?
How does he treat Chelsea?
What does she do to change him from being cross to being friendly?
What would you do if you were Chelsea and you met an ogre?

Can you think of a new name for Lonely?

Writing task

Write a different ending to the story.

Write a new story about what happened next.

Art task

Draw or paint an ogre.

Use papier mâché to make a model of an ogre.

Books

The Ogre of Oglefort, Eva Ibbotson
Ogres Don't Hunt Easter Eggs, Debbie Dadey, Marcia Thornton Jones & John Steven Gurney

Text and grammar

Look at the text of the story:

How do you know when someone is speaking?
How do you know when a question is being asked?
Find the question marks.
Can you write a question to ask Chelsea?
Can you find an ellipsis? Why and when do we use ellipses?

Writing task

Write a conversation between Chelsea and Lonely using speech marks, question marks and ellipsis.

Use of words as illustrations

Look at the words 'grin', 'shook', 'jumped' and 'downstairs' in the book and how they have been made to look like the meaning of the word. Can you think of another word to do this with? (For example, leapt, sank, curved.)

IT and art task

On the computer, type a word to show its meaning (like the word 'jumped' in the book).

Draw a word that shows its meaning like the words 'grin' and 'shook' in the book.

Bold and Fonts

Can you find some bold print in the book? Why do we use bold print?
Look at the fonts. How many different fonts can you find?

Why has the author used different fonts?

Writing and IT task

Write a paragraph about something that has happened in school using bold print to show emphasis and different fonts that help to express the meaning of words.

Circle Time

Behaviour, inclusion and friendship discussion

Key questions:

What did Chelsea do that was not good behaviour in the classroom?

How could she change her behaviour?

Have you ever done anything that was not good behaviour in school?

What did you do to change your behaviour?

Why is Chelsea lonely?

What could she do that would help her make friends?

What could the other children do to help her make friends?

What happens in the story that we wouldn't want to happen to anyone in our class?

How can we make sure these things don't happen?

OUR STREET
BOOKS

Our Street Books for children of all ages, deliver a potent mix of
fantastic, rip-roaring adventure and fantasy stories to excite the
imagination; spiritual fiction to help the mind and the heart
grow; humorous stories to make the funny bone grow; historical
tales to evolve interest; and all manner of subjects that stretch
imagination, grab attention, inform, inspire and keep the pages
turning. Our subjects include Non-fiction and Fiction, Fantasy
and Science Fiction, Religious, Spiritual, Historical, Adventure,
Social Issues, Humour, Folk Tales and more.